Madelyn Butterfly
and
Emma Cricket
Wing It

Written by Cathy Cress Eller
Illustrated by Juan Carlos Colla

ISBN 978-1-936352-27-2
1-936352-27-3

Published by Mirror Publishing
Milwaukee, WI 53214

Printed in the USA.

This book is dedicated to my dear friend, Lynne, who is also my outstanding personal editor. She listens, supports, laughs, and always has an extra comma when I need one. Thank you Lynne!

Emma Cricket was going for her morning hop to visit her dear friend, Madelyn Butterfly. It was a warm, blue-sky day and there was just a hint of a breeze in the trees.

She chirped her best cricket song as she hopped past Carnella Caterpillar's house and she waved to Ruby & Rodney (the twin fireflies) as they buzzed their favorite lavender flowers.

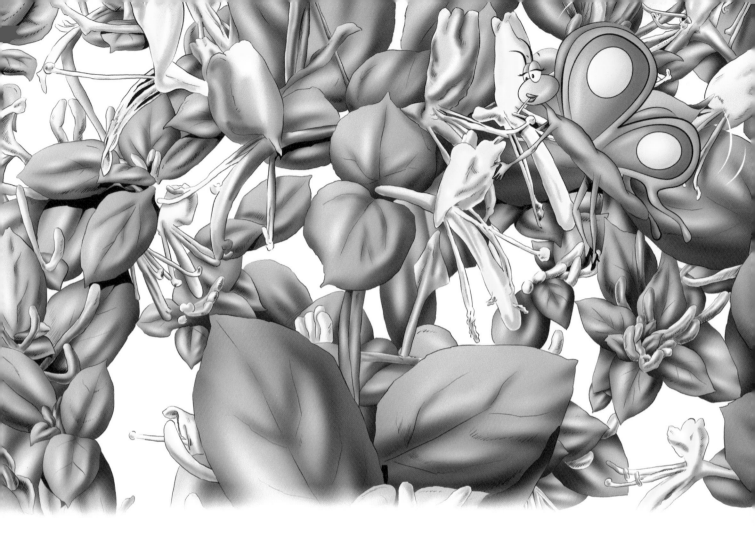

She saw Ladybug Grace chatting with Owen Ant and Cecil Carpenter Ant at the flower garden pool.

When Emma arrived at Madelyn's house, she was collecting nectar from her honeysuckle blossoms.

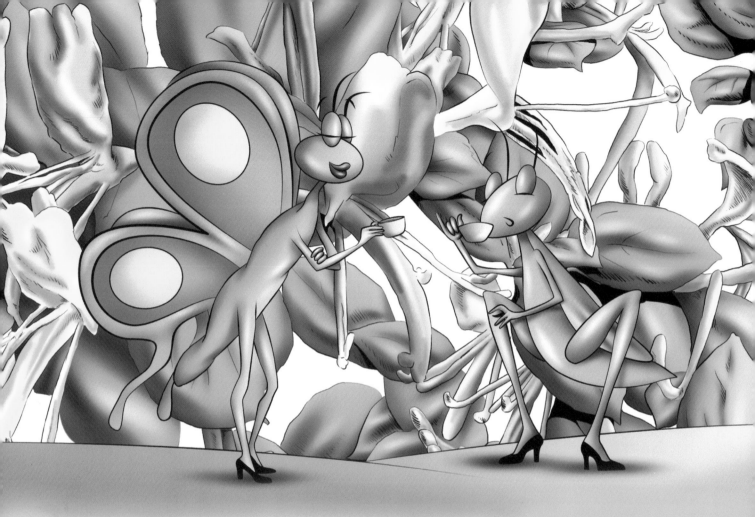

"Good morning Emma, I've been collecting honeysuckle nectar all morning. Would you like some warm honeysuckle tea?" asked Madelyn.

"Oh, that would taste yummy after my long hop," Emma chirped. She took a long sip of the honeysuckle tea. "Oh, Madelyn, I do believe this is the best honeysuckle tea I've ever had!" declared Emma.

Madelyn beamed with pride and whispered, "It is tasty, if I do say so myself."

"It's a beautiful blue-sky day and I wondered if you might like to go for a hop and fly?"asked Emma.

Madelyn flittered her wings and said, "That sounds like buggity fun. Where would you like to go?"

"Well, you know, the Little Baja path is nice this time of year. We can hop and fly there," suggested Emma.

So Madelyn fluttered her wings as Emma hopped and they headed to the Little Baja path. When they reached the path, it was not grassy and colorful as they remembered.

Madelyn hovered above the briars and brambles and said, "What has happened to the Little Baja path? It used to be so lovely."

Emma struggled to hop in the tangle of briars and brambles. "Maybe the path will be easier if we go a little farther," chirped Emma.

But the farther Madelyn flew and the farther Emma hopped, the more tangled the briars and brambles became. All at once, Emma gave a frightening chirp, "I can't hop Madelyn, I'm stuck! I can't get out. Oh, I wish I could fly like you!"

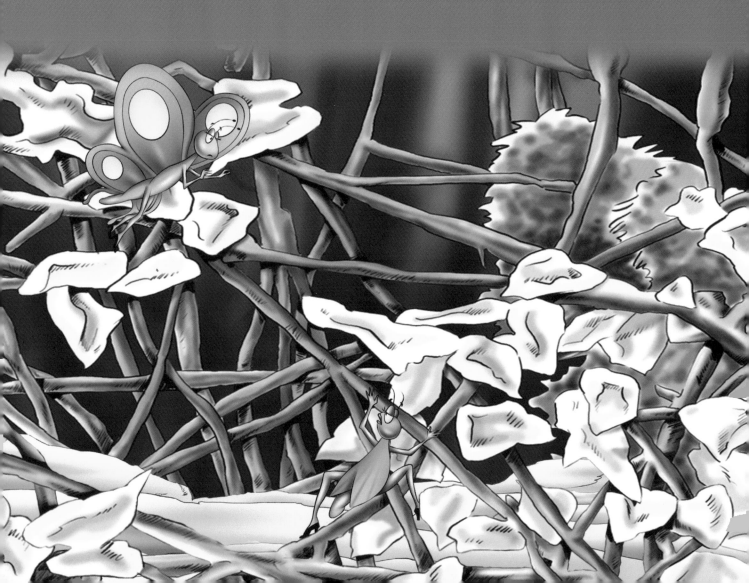

Madelyn hovered low and saw that Emma was indeed tangled deep in the briars and brambles on the path. "I'm going to try to flutter my wings very hard and see if I can move the briars and brambles with a breeze from above," said Madelyn.

"Ok," whimpered Emma.

Madelyn spread her wings wide and soared with the breeze as fast as she could. She fluttered, flapped and quivered her wings and the brambles swayed ever so slightly, but the briars did not move at all. "Maybe you could chew through the briars and brambles," Madelyn suggested to Emma.

"They are too thick to chew. How will I ever get out?" cried Emma.

All the while, Madelyn was thinking and circling high above Emma and then she had an amazing idea. Madelyn flew as low and close to Emma as she could, and in her softest, calmest voice she said, "Emma, I can't get you out, but you can fly like me and you can get out!"

"No, I can't!" screeched Emma.

"Yes, you can, Emma," reassured Madelyn. "You have wings that you've never used. You keep them tucked away because it's easier for you to hop."

"But I've never used them before. I can't do it!" sobbed Emma.

"Emma, we all have talents and gifts we don't use, maybe it's time you untuck your wings and give them a try," Madelyn said with encouragement. "You can do it, Emma! You can do it, Emma!" Madelyn began to cheer.

Emma began to fidget in the briars and brambles. "I don't even know if they will unfold, Madelyn, but I'll try," she said with a sniffle.

"Just slowly unfold one wing at a time and wiggle them a little bit," Madelyn said.

"I'll try," grunted Emma, as she slowly wiggled each wing.

"Now, carefully stretch them all the way out like this," Madelyn said as she stretched her own wings.

"Ok, I am," said Emma with a little quiver in her voice.

"Emma, now I want you to slowly move them little by little," instructed Madelyn.

"I'm doing it!" Emma squealed with delight.
"Now move them a little faster," Madelyn instructed again.
"I'm fluttering, I'm fluttering!" chirped Emma.

"Now, flutter them faster and faster. You can do it! You can do it!" Madelyn coached.

About that time, Emma soared right out of the briars and brambles to where Madelyn was hovering.

"I knew you could do it!" cheered Madelyn as she congratulated Emma on her courageous escape and newly discovered gift....her wings!

The pine trees swayed and seemed to wave good-bye as they both flew back to the flower garden pool to tell everyone about their adventure. First, they saw Ladybug Grace chatting with Carnella at the mint patch and said, "Follow us to the garden pool."

So Ladybug Grace and Carnella quickly followed them. Next, they saw Ruby and Rodney napping under the holly bush. "Wake up quick, and meet us at the garden pool," Carnella whispered as she rolled past them. Owen and Cecil were floating in the garden pool when all the other bugs arrived.

"Looks like a bug parade coming around the sliding stone," said Owen as he waved to all his friends.

"What's all the chatter about?" Cecil asked, as he climbed out of the garden pool.

They all gathered around and eagerly awaited the big news.

Emma took a deep breath and announced, "I found a very special gift today!"

"What was it? Where is it? Where did you find it?" all the bugs buzzed at once.

"Well, it isn't an ordinary gift," grinned Emma. Then she told all her buggy buddies about their adventure in the briars and brambles and how Madelyn helped her find her hidden gift, the ability to use her wings.

They all laughed and cheered and told Emma how proud they were of her.

Emma looked at Madelyn and said, "Thank you for helping me to realize that I had a gift I had never used." After a thoughtful moment, Emma's eyes grew wide and she looked at Madelyn and said, "Madelyn, you have a special gift too!"

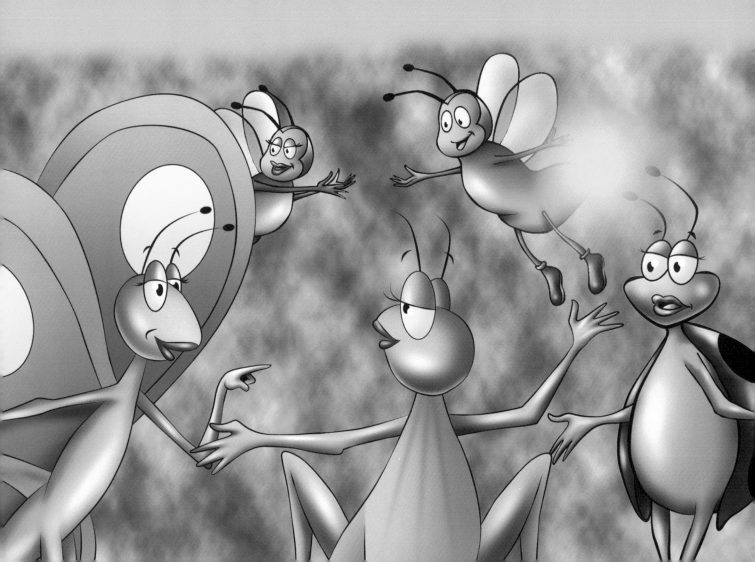

"And what might that gift be?" grinned Madelyn.

"You encouraged me with kind and patient words. You cheered me on to use my wings until I did it. You taught me that I could do something I didn't know I could do. That is a very special gift!"

Carnella said, "You're right, Emma, that is a special gift indeed."

"You know, Ruby said shyly, we all have hidden gifts and talents. Sometimes, it takes a frightful situation, like Emma getting caught in the briars and brambles, to make us pull from way down deep inside to do things that we didn't know we could do."

"Sometimes it just takes a little help from your friends," beamed Emma as she hugged Madelyn tight.

All the buggy buddies stretched out on the warm sliding stone and chattered into the evening. Each one wondered about their own hidden gifts and talents.

**EVERYONE HAS SPECIAL GIFTS AND TALENTS
HAVE YOU DISCOVERED YOURS?**

CPSIA information can be obtained
at www.ICGtesting.com
Printed in the USA
259691LV00002B